BY EMILY L. HAY HINSDALE · ILLUSTRATED BY

FLY FISHING
ESCAPING THE RAGING RIVER

WILDERNESS ADVENTURES

FOR MY DAD, ALWAYS MY VOICE IN THE WILDERNESS – ELH
TO MY PARENTS, PETER AND LEANNE – CO

Fly Fishing: Escaping the Raging River

Published by Bakken Books. Copyright © 2023 by Abdo Consulting Group, Inc. International copyrights reserved in all countries. No part of this book may be reproduced in any form without written permission from the publisher.

This book is published by agreement with Abdo Books.

ISBN 978-1-955657-83-9
For Worldwide Distribution
Printed in the U.S.A.

Written by Emily L. Hay Hinsdale
Illustrated by Caitlin O'Dwyer
Edited by Tamara L. Britton
Art Directed by Candice Keimig

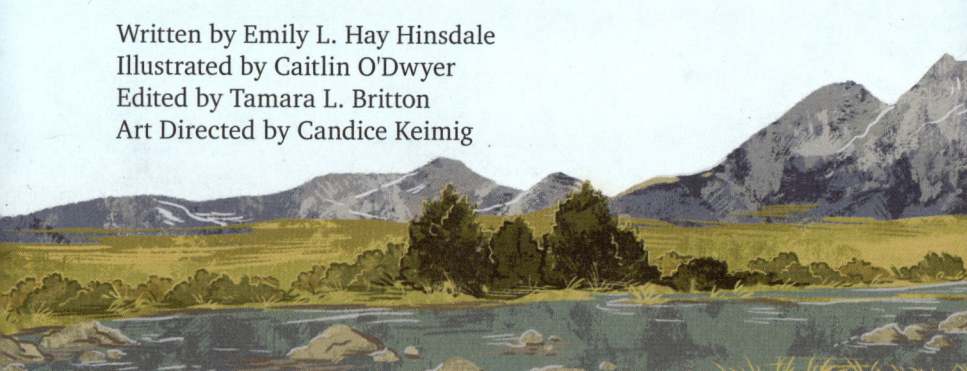

TABLE OF CONTENTS

CHAPTER 1
GONE FISHIN'. 4

CHAPTER 2
HITTING THE TRAIL 16

CHAPTER 3
LURED AWAY. 28

CHAPTER 4
FLY AND FLY AGAIN 38

CHAPTER 5
OF PARENTS AND PLANS 50

CHAPTER 6
CAUGHT! 62

CHAPTER 7
IN A FLASH 72

CHAPTER 8
SMELLS LIKE WET DOG 84

CHAPTER 9
IT'S GEOLOGY 92

CHAPTER 10
HUGS AND FISHES 104

CHAPTER 1
GONE FISHIN'

Seb woke up with the tip of his brand new fly fishing rod tickling his ear. There wasn't quite room for it in the tent, but he had wanted it next to him so he could be totally ready to fish the first chance he got.

Across the tent, he could hear his stepsister, Sami, stirring in her sleeping bag, too. He put his glasses on and peered over at her just in time to see her reach out a hand to touch her own fly rod, next to her suitcase. Someone else was just as ready as he was to get fishing.

Seb sat up and pulled on a sweatshirt. Sami sat up, too, and smiled at him. Together, moving quietly so as not to wake up the parents, they crept out of the tent.

Outside, it was early morning, bright and clear. Seb looked up at the high mountains ahead of them. Big, purple mountains rising suddenly out of the forests below, where they were camping. This was Wyoming's Bridger-Teton National Forest, where they would all camp and fish for the next week.

"Did you know . . ." Seb started to say, but Sami interrupted him.

"That's the Wind River Range," Sami told Seb. "Part of the Grand Tetons, which are part of the whole Rocky Mountain range that stretches up the middle of Wyoming."

Seb knew that. He had read all about these mountains in the book on Wyoming that he'd gotten from the library before the trip along with a book on fly fishing. He'd read both two times already and couldn't wait to see those mountains come to life in front of him—evergreen forests, wildflower fields, and crystal clear streams that would be, he hoped, full of fish.

"Did you know that there are mainly two kinds of fish that we can catch in the river we're going to camp on? Brook trout, mostly, but maybe also some rainbow trout," Seb said.

"Brookies!" said Sami. "Real fishermen call them brookies."

Seb sighed. Sami was always full of firsthand information about fishing and hunting and anything outdoors. And she was always ready to share that information with Seb.

He looked sideways at Sami as she zipped up her hoodie and started toward the family's Jeep, parked under a couple of big pine trees. At home, Sami was quiet and pretty easy to get along with, for a fifteen-year-old girl. Seb had been excited about having a family with a sibling when his mom, Kathleen, had married Sami's dad, Carlos, last year. And most of the time, Seb didn't mind at all having an older sister.

Most of the time. The rest of the time, he really wished she could just be not quite so good at everything, especially when it came to camping and hunting and fishing. Sami had been on outdoor adventures with Carlos since she was really little.

Now it seemed like she knew everything about the wilderness and Seb could never catch up, no matter how many books he read. It wasn't like he was a little kid that Sami should be babysitting. He was thirteen, only two years younger than she was, and he was a getting tired of having Sami show him what to do.

Behind him, Seb heard the tent flap unzip and he turned around to see Kathleen and

Carlos crawling out. Suddenly, they were shoved to the side and a wild, red golden retriever burst out of the tent between them and ran to Seb, tail and ears flapping wildly.

"Rocky!" Seb said to the dog, laughing. "Don't run over your family!"

Carlos climbed out of the tent and offered a hand to Kathleen to pull her up. "The teenagers are up early, the dog can't contain himself . . . I think some people are excited to get fishing. Right, Seb?"

He patted Seb on the back and Seb nodded. He *was* excited to get fishing. He even had his own fishing license. Though he wasn't old enough to need one, Sami pointed out that forteen was the age limit. But with his own, then he could catch as many fish as were allowed. If he caught any at all.

"Well if everyone's this excited to go," Kathleen said. "Everyone can get to work striking this camp and packing up for our pack in."

"We can leave right after breakfast!" Sami said.

Sami and Seb together ran at the tent and started rolling up sleeping bags. Rocky followed them and got in the way jumping on top of everything they were trying to do. They needed to get everything rolled up and stowed carefully, because all of it had to be loaded into packs.

The night before, they had camped next to the Jeep near a ranger station. But the rest of the trip was going to be a different kind of camping than Seb had tried before.

Other trips with Carlos and Sami had been car camping, with the car right there next to the campground, full of all the food and tents and sleeping bags they needed. But for this trip, they would be leaving the Jeep behind and hiking deeper into the forest than any car could go, carrying all of their supplies in backpacks.

Sami carried her sleeping bag and air mattress to the Jeep and started attaching them to her backpack. Rocky pranced around her, ready to play.

"Someone's ready to hike," Sami laughed. "I wonder if he'll be as enthusiastic when he finds out he has to wear a pack, too."

Seb wasn't too sure how thrilled he was to wear a pack either. It sounded like hard work.

"I've got all my clothes stowed already," Sami said. "I'm leaving room in the top to add in some of the food."

"I can take some food, too," Seb said. "It can go on top of my books."

"Books?" Sami stared at him. "You're not

seriously going to carry all the extra weight of those books while we're hiking, are you?"

Seb stared back at her. "If you don't have books to read, what do you when you're sitting around the camp? And how do you know about the mountains and the fish and everything? Our phones won't get service, so we won't be able to look stuff up."

Sami rolled her eyes. "You just know stuff before you go," she said.

"Do you know how to tell the difference between a brown trout and a brook trout?" Seb said. "They have different colored spots on their bodies."

"Fine," Sami said. "You read. I'll be fishing."

She patted the pocket of her pack, which contained a collection of "flies," the fish hooks decorated with feathers and thread that fly fishermen used to lure trout to the surface from the deep pools in the river.

Kathleen and Carlos had gotten breakfast ready while Sami and Seb were packing. Everyone ate quickly and it didn't take long before they were all at work taking the tent down and getting packed. They all wanted to get started on the hike right away, so they could find their camping place up river early in the day.

The packs were mostly already full. Clothes had been tightly rolled and shoved to the bottom of the packs before they all left home. The lightweight dried food and snacks had been shared around among all of their bags so that everyone carried some of it.

Sleeping bags and air mattresses were now strapped to the outside of the packs. Kathleen had tied a few pots and pans to her pack for cooking. Carlos would carry the portable camp stove. They all carried their own rods. Which left only one item.

"Rocky!" Carlos called. "Are you ready for your pack?"

Rocky had been sniffing around while they prepared. Hearing his name, he looked up at Carlos. Carlos was holding a backpack made for dogs and Rocky recognized it— and didn't like it. He tried to hide behind Sami, but Carlos grabbed him by the collar.

"Sorry, Rocky, old buddy," Carlos said. "But this is a family trip and we all have to do our part."

The pack buckled around Rocky's chest and belly, with two small pouches hanging on either side of his back. His food was stowed in the pouches. He might not need clothes or fishing lures or books, but he would need dinner!

Rocky tried to bite at the pack, turning around in circles. Then he gave himself a little shake and, rubbing his nose against Carlos's hand, took off running toward the trail.

Seb joined the rest of the family laughing at their wild dog. He took a good look at his

own pack. If Rocky could do it, so could he. He leaned the pack against the back of the Jeep, slipped the straps over his shoulders and hoisted it onto his back, bobbling a little under the sudden weight. He buckled the waist strap around his middle, and pulled his fishing rod from the back of the Jeep.

He felt a little unsteady, but he wiggled the pack on his back until he felt more secure. He was going to pack in his own camping gear and he was going to fish. He may not be an expert like Sami, but he was ready.

CHAPTER 2
HITTING THE TRAIL

Ready or not, once the hike got started, Seb did not enjoy carrying that heavy pack. With the waist strap to help support it, not all of the weight hung on his shoulders, but they still felt pushed down and uncomfortable.

His legs felt slow and uncoordinated. His hair, which tended to stick out in wild curls, kept catching at the top of the pack.

He tried to swing his arms but that only made the pack feel more awkward. Also, the tip of his fly rod dipped into the dirt as he swung it. He hastily pulled it up straight, hoping Sami hadn't noticed.

Rocky, running ahead of them, didn't seem to be enjoying his pack either. He kept stopping every now and then to rub his back against a tree, trying to scrape the pack off. Carlos had buckled it on well, though.

"No luck, Rocky," Seb said to Rocky quietly as he passed the dog leaning against a tree. "We both have to do this. This is camping."

Their first stop was at the ranger station. The door was locked and they couldn't see a ranger anywhere around.

"I don't think we'll wait," Carlos said. "It's not my first time up here, so I don't need directions. I'll put our names and where we plan to go in the registration book so they know where to find us. But I want to get moving. We have three miles to hike before we get to the area where I want to set up camp."

"Three miles isn't far," said Sami, cheerfully.

"You'll think it's pretty far when you've

climbed a mountainside wearing a pack that big," her dad told her.

Three miles sounded plenty far to Seb.

The trailhead started off with an even and easy stretch through a pine wood. Seb could hear wind whispering through the top of the tall, swaying pines. He heard another sound behind it. Something tinkling.

Kathleen heard it, too. "Is that running water I hear?" she asked.

"Yes, the river is just up ahead. We'll see it when the trail dips down," Carlos told her.

"Did you know we have to cross the river over and over again on this hike?" Seb asked. "Carlos showed me the map and the trail winds around a lot. Crossing a river is called 'fording.'"

"If Rocky gets into the water, it's just called wet," Sami said. "He loves to swim and then he'll shake all over us."

The trail suddenly started to slope downward. The trees changed from pines to willows and aspen, and grasses and wildflowers were growing among them. It was easy to tell, even if Seb hadn't read about changes in vegetation, that they were coming closer to water. Everything just looked wetter.

They turned a bend in the trail and there was the Sweetwater River in front of them. It wasn't a huge river, though Seb knew from his Wyoming book that it flowed down through the mountain range and out into the plains. By then, it would have gathered enough water from tributaries to be wider and deeper. Here it was more of a stream, bright in the sunshine, darting between shallow rocks.

"It's beautiful," Kathleen exclaimed.

"Did you know it's called the Sweetwater

because its water is clear and fresh and lots of early pioneers in this area liked to drink it? But we have to boil it or use a water filter before we can drink it because now we know it can contain parasites," Seb said.

Rocky was already prancing along the shallows, splashing water everywhere.

"Come on, Rocky," Carlos called. "You'll have plenty of time to play in the river after we get to our camp."

He led the way along the riverbank to where a log bridge—just three logs rolled together—had been built across the river. Seb stepped across it cautiously, feeling his legs unsteady on the uneven surface and his pack shifting his weight.

Across the river, the trail climbed steeply back into the woods. The trail followed the river, but mostly from a ridge above it. This is where the serious hiking began.

They were about a mile into their hike and starting to feel how heavy the packs were, when they were stopped by a shout from ahead of them. Seb looked up to see a man on a horse coming down the trail toward them.

"Howdy, folks!" the man called. As he came closer, Seb could see he was dressed in a forest ranger uniform. "Looks like you're heading out for some serious camping." The man smiled down at Seb, looking at his fishing rod. "And fishing."

"Is that OK?" Seb asked.

The man laughed. His face was a dark tan and crinkled around the eyes. "Fine by me," he said.

"Good to see you, ranger," Carlos said. "We stopped by the ranger station at the trailhead. I left our names, but we wanted to get going while it was still light out."

"Good idea," the ranger said. "Do you have a campsite in mind?"

Carlos described a big meadow and a camping spot near it between two lakes. Seb didn't see how anyone could understand where that was, but the ranger nodded.

"That's a great fishing spot," he said. "Just make sure you keep your camp well above the riverbank. We've had a lot of rain this summer, more than usual. The ground is wet and we've been experiencing some flash flooding when it rains in the mountains. Nothing dangerous, but you don't want to camp in it!"

"Flash floods can turn dangerous pretty quickly," said Kathleen. "Are you sure we should be camping near the river?"

"We'll make sure we're well away from the water and we'll keep an eye on the weather," Carlos said to Kathleen and the ranger. "As long as the flooding doesn't worry the fish, it doesn't worry us!"

The ranger laughed. "Good luck with those fish, then," he said.

They stepped off the trail to make room for his horse to pass them and they started hiking again.

Seb hiked slowly, trying to think of what he had read about flash floods. It wasn't like regular flooding where there was a lot of rain and the water level slowly rose. Flash floods were just like they sounded—they happened in a flash.

When the ground was really wet or really dry so it couldn't absorb a lot of water all at once, a big rainstorm would send a ton of water down a stream or river. It could happen in just a few minutes sometimes.

Seb pictured himself fishing along the river and the water suddenly rising. He wasn't even sure what he would do. He reminded himself to discuss this with Carlos. He also reminded himself to ask Carlos what fish did when the river flooded.

Sami shouted up ahead and Seb brought his mind back to the trail and the hike.

"Next river ford!" she said.

This ford didn't have a bridge, even a log one. The river was shallow here and dotted with lots of rocks.

"Do we wade?" Kathleen asked.

"We rock hop!" Sami shouted. She stepped out onto a rock in the river and then to another one, using the rocks as a natural path across the water.

"It's not too bad," Carlos said. "There are plenty of rocks to step on. If you happen to miss one, the water is only a few inches deep here." He pointed downriver. "Not like down there."

Seb followed his hand to see that past the ford, the river turned, widening and deepening into a large pool, overhung with grass and willows.

"Did you know pools like that are a good place to look for fish?" Seb asked excitedly. He hurried over to look down into the pool, hoping to spot a fish hovering in the deep water.

"Watch out!" Carlos yelled.

Seb looked around just in time to see a rush of red fur as Rocky ran past him and jumped into the water.

The splash was tremendous. It went all over Seb and sent little waves upstream to the ford, where it washed over the toes of Sami's hiking boots.

"Rocky!" they all shouted.

And then Seb spotted that Rocky wasn't swimming well. The dog backpack was

waterproof and it floated to the surface; it was pushing forward over Rocky's head as the dog tried to keep his nose and eyes above water.

Rocky's head was being pushed under water.

CHAPTER 3
LURED AWAY

"I'm coming, Rocky!" Seb shouted.

Rocky paddled with his big front paws as hard as he could, but he couldn't shift the pack from his back.

Quickly, Seb worked to remove his own pack. He staggered, almost falling backward as he wiggled his shoulders out from under the straps. He dropped his fishing rod and pushed the pack off.

"Come here, Rocky," he said.

He flung himself belly first on the riverbank and stretched out his arms into the pool. He could just catch the edge of Rocky's pack with his fingers. He grabbed at it, dragging it—and the struggling dog— toward him.

As he pulled, a buckle on the pack snapped open. Rocky kicked and it was free from his back. He lunged sputtering toward the riverbank and Seb let go of the pack to grab hold of the dog's collar. Rocky scrambled over the edge of the bank and fell

on top of Seb, shaking himself and licking Seb's face.

"Ew, Rocky, not my glasses!" Seb said laughing. He was soaked, but relieved.

Carlos had taken his pack off, too, and come running down the path to them both.

"This is why Rocky is not the world's best fishing dog," he said, looking down at the wet dog and Seb. "You both okay?"

Seb nodded and sat up, wiping his glasses off on his wet shirt.

"Hey!" Sami's voice came from the opposite riverbank. "I found Rocky's pack!"

The pack had drifted downstream in the current. It was stuck in some branches just below the pool and Sami had climbed down the bank to retrieve it.

Seb and Carlos retrieved their own packs and other gear and finally forded the stream to join Kathleen and Sami on the other side of the river. Sami bent to buckle the dog pack back on Rocky. He hung his head sadly.

"You almost lost all your food, Rocky," Sami said. "You wouldn't have liked that, would you?"

Three miles is a long way walking down a flat city street. It's a really long way when you wind up and down the ridges along a mountain river carrying a heavy pack on your back.

Whenever they stopped to rest, Seb sat on top of a log, leaning into it so the log would prop up the pack's weight and give his back and shoulders a rest.

It was early afternoon as they paused above a rocky canyon to look down at the river as it dashed and gurgled in a series of splashy leaps over rocks and the deep pools between them. Beyond the canyon, the riverbanks leveled out and the river flowed through a small pine forest before stretching out in a big wide meadow.

"End of the trail for us!" Carlos said.

"Where do we camp? Not on this ridge, surely," said Kathleen.

"Down in that pine forest just above the meadow," said Carlos, pointing. "You can't quite see the spot from here."

"Which is good," Sami said. "I don't want a bunch of people hiking by to see our camp."

"How do we get there?" Seb asked. "There's no trail."

"We make our own!" Sami said. She headed off on the side of the trail, pushing her way through some grasses and underbrush toward the river. Seb followed her in a winding path down the ridge and into the meadow below.

Here the river broke into many channels. Some of them were narrow enough to hop over, some could be crossed on rocks, and some had to be waded. But this was their last ford before they made camp and settled down to enjoy the river as a neighbor.

Seb didn't mind getting his feet wet now that they were close to stopping. He squelched through water and mud and was happy when Sami led the way up out of the meadow and into the forest.

"Great spot!" Kathleen called from behind them.

The campsite had was in the center of a clearing among the trees. There was a firepit in the center. An ancient tree had fallen across one end. It was so old that all the bark had fallen away; it would make a wonderful bench for them to sit on and a great place to set up the camp stove.

Sami was already leaning back against the log to wiggle out of her backpack. "Let's set everything up really fast so we can get fishing!" she said.

Seb sighed to himself. Sami was always rushing ahead and faster at everything than he was. He wasn't sure he was that anxious to start fishing. What if he couldn't do it?

But with his pack off, he felt a little more energetic. His shoulders felt so light, that it was almost as though he could float away. Carlos had pulled the tent off his pack and Sami and Seb started emptying out the tent bag to get it set up.

There was a lot to be done to get a camp set up. The tent had to be put together and sleeping bags and clothes stored inside. Food was gathered into one pack and Carlos hoisted it up over a tree branch so bears could not get into it. Wood had to be gathered for the fire. The camp stove had to be set up. Water had to be fetched from the river.

With Sami hustling them along, however, the camp came together faster than Seb would have thought possible. Sami kept stopping to inspect her fishing rod and every time she did, Seb felt nervous.

"Well," said Carlos, looking around at their camp. "The sun will set soon, but I think we're ready for the night. All that's left to do is go check out the river for good fishing spots. Sami and Seb, do you think you could handle that?"

Sami grinned. "I think we can, Dad."

She grabbed her rod. Rocky jumped to go with her.

"No thanks, fishing dog," she said. "You've had enough water time today."

Rocky lay back down and looked depressed. Seb patted his head and tried not to look the same. He got his rod, too, and followed behind Sami as she cut through the pine trees back to the river bank.

Sami, of course, had several flies already attached to her jacket. When they got to the riverbank, she started sorting through them.

"It always takes a little while to figure out the best lure," she said.

"I read in my book that brook trout—brookies—really like to eat flies so you should use a lure that looks like them," Seb said.

"Maybe. If there are a lot of different bugs around this area. We'll find out. You have to just do it, not read about it," she said.

She stepped out into the river. The line, dancing on the end of her rod, swished a few times about her head and then shot out past her, the lure dropping delicately into the river like a fly landing on the water. She let it settle there for a moment, and then pulled it back up, swirling in the air again.

Seb blinked. He'd practiced at home in their backyard with Carlos. Could he do it now? Like Sami did?

He gathered the line in his hand and pulled his rod up. The lure sailed into the air with it and he moved his arm quickly in the back-and-forth motion he'd learned from his stepfather. And now it was time to release. He let the line soar out over the water.

Except that it didn't.

Seb looked over his shoulder. The line was stuck in a tree, snagged on a low branch.

From down the river, he heard laughter. He turned around to see Sami watching him and giggling.

"That always happens to people who don't know much about fishing," she said.

CHAPTER 4
FLY AND FLY AGAIN

Seb glared at her. "I'm sure it has never happened to you," he said sarcastically.

Sami tossed her braids over her shoulders. "Maybe, when I was first learning how to fish. A long time ago."

Seb turned his back at her and pushed his glasses into place. They tended to slide down his nose when he was excited or upset. He untangled the fishing line and hook from the branch and then looked over his shoulder. Sami had gone back to fishing. She wasn't watching him. He'd give it another try.

His second cast caught on the branches again. He moved a little away from them. The next cast went out toward the river, like it should, but landed in the rocks on the river bank. The third cast snagged in some underbrush on the opposite side of the river. He tugged on the line, but it was stuck firmly. The light was fading, but he could just see the fly, a little tuft of fur and thread, caught on a piece of driftwood.

"Sami! Seb! It's getting dark! Time to come back to camp and have dinner,"

Kathleen's voice, calling behind him, made him jump. He could hear Sami coming back up the river bank. He gave another strong tug on the line and it popped free and he pulled it back in. Only the line came back across the water, though. The fly was still snagged on the driftwood and he was left with only a broken line.

"Hey," said Sami. "Did you catch anything?"

"No," Seb said. He wasn't about to add

that he'd almost caught some driftwood.

"Yeah, me neither," said Sami. "But I'm sure I will tomorrow."

She seemed really happy to be fishing. Seb was envious of how Sami seemed to just fit right in every time they were in the wilderness. He never felt that way.

The next morning, Seb woke up with lots of energy, ready to try fishing again. He'd read through his fly fishing book again by the light of the tent lantern before he fell asleep. He thought through all the arm positions in his mind, where his wrist needed to turn to send a cast out over the water to the right spot.

"Sami," he said as they were crawling out of the tent into the morning sun. "Did you know that trout like to hang out in those little pools in the river because that's where stuff like flies and moths can land for them to eat?"

"Seb, is there anything you can't find in a book?" Sami asked him, laughing.

How to actually make the fishing line do what I want, Seb thought.

After breakfast, they were both back at the river. Sami was determined to present Kathleen with her full daily limit of fish to fry up for dinner. She had a whole series of flies hooked to her jacket. Seb didn't even know the names of all of them.

Sami confidently selected a fly and attached it to her line. She had already started down to the river's edge before Seb had his line ready.

OK, today he was going to do this. Seb attached a new fly to the end of his line leader. The leader was a light piece of line that attached to the end of the longer, heavier fishing line.

The fishing line was supposed to be heavy enough to get it to sail out across the water. The leader was light enough to let the fly itself just float onto the river's surface, like a real insect landing on the water. This was dry fly fishing, perfect for shallow mountain streams.

Seb let the heavy fishing line and lure play out a bit and then started flicking his arm back and forth, back and forth. That was the right motion. He could do this.

He actually got a good cast off on the fourth try. A fish didn't bite, but he didn't expect it to right away. He went closer to the water, balancing on some rocks to get himself closer to a pool that formed at a bend in the river. He flipped the line up, back, and over, almost to the bank and into the shadows. He saw a dart of movement under the water. He leaned forward, and then . . .

Splash!

Seb had slipped off the rocks and fallen into the water. Waves splashed up on the banks and sent ripples washing downstream. Seb sat up, soaked head to toe in icy water. It dripped down from his curly hair and ran over his glasses.

"Seb!" Sami yelled. "What are you doing?! You spoiled the hole!"

Seb scrambled out of the water clutching his fishing rod to see Sami storming up the riverbank toward him.

"You ruined the fishing for this whole area," Sami said. "Do you think fish are going to hang around when you've scared them like that?"

44

"I fell," Seb protested.

"You should have been more careful," Sami said, glaring at him.

Seb had had enough. He was wet, cold, and he didn't think he'd ever be able to catch a fish.

"It's not like you were catching any fish

anyway," Seb yelled at her. "I don't think you're really such an expert."

He pushed past her, stomping back into the river. It was only deep enough to go over his already wet ankles in the rocky area above the pool. He splashed across, water squelching in his shoes.

Seb heard Sami call his name behind him, but he didn't answer. He was ready for a break from fishing and a break from her.

Across the river, he climbed hard and fast up the bank to the ridge above it, panting as he went. Sami could fish without him. She was the expert anyway.

Reaching the top of the ridge, he turned upstream. The ridge kept getting higher and he realized he was now by the canyon they'd seen yesterday when hiking in. Down below, he could see how the river tossed over rocks and then slowed into deep eddies.

That would be a perfect place to fish, Seb thought. The canyon wasn't too narrow. There was still room for a fisherman to stand on the rocky shore and cast into the pools. It was a perfect, private place. He could get in some practice without Sami's advice.

Seb walked back down to the river feeling much better. Sami was no longer by the riverbank when he waded across, but his fishing rod was still there. He picked it up and made his way back to the camp.

"Hi Seb," said Kathleen as he walked into the camp. She was sitting in the shade reading a book. Carlos and Sami were nowhere in sight.

"Hi," he said.

"You look wetter than a fish," she said.

"I know Sami told you I fell in," Seb said, frowning.

"Yes, she did," Kathleen answered with a smile. "I'll bet that was a surprise."

"She didn't have to yell at me about it," Seb said.

"Hmm," Kathleen stood up and walked over to him. She had a towel in her hand and gave his head a good rub with it. His hair stood straight up. "You know, Sami has been fishing and camping a long time. You and I are still pretty new to this."

Seb didn't say anything. Sami didn't make fun of Kathleen for not being an expert camper.

"You know that all new things take practice to learn. Like reading. You're so good at that, but you wouldn't have been if you didn't keep working on it," Kathleen said.

"Mom," Seb said. "I think you're being a little obvious with the moral of the story."

Kathleen laughed and gently pushed his glasses back up his nose. "Carlos and Sami and Rocky went to look for wild blueberries near the meadow. I think I'll go join them. Want to come?"

Seb shook his head. "I'm alright here," he said.

Kathleen sighed. "Well, I guess you can stay here alone in the camp. But no more wandering off on your own, OK? Even if you're mad at your stepsister, heading off on your own isn't such a good idea."

"OK," Seb said. He didn't need to wander off. He was going to practice his casting right here in the camp until he got the motion back, like he had at home. And then tomorrow, he was going to fish the canyon—out of Sami's sight.

CHAPTER 5
OF PARENTS AND PLANS

Of course, plans never work out like you think they will when there are parents around.

"You absolutely cannot go fish some canyon by yourself," Kathleen said the next morning.

"But, Mom . . ." Seb said.

"Your mom is right about buddying up when you're out in the wilderness," Carlos said. "You never know when having someone else around will be important. How about this—Sami can go with you!"

Seb groaned inside. Sami did not look that pleased either.

"I only caught three fish yesterday, Dad," Sami said. "I need to be serious about it today."

"Fine," Carlos said. "Be serious about it in the canyon with Seb. That canyon will be a great place to fish. You two stay together. I'm going to take Kathleen to a little lake on the other side of the meadow to see if we can catch some big cutthroat trout, so you kids will be on your own."

Sami's groan was not inside. Seb kicked the dirt, but didn't say anything.

"Take Rocky with you," suggested Kathleen. "Everyone likes hanging out with Rocky."

Rocky had been lying in the shade by the tent. Hearing his name, he jumped up and stood there, wagging his tail vigorously.

"OK, you can come, Rocky," said Sami, laughing at him.

Rocky ran over to her and leaned against her, his tongue hanging out of his mouth. *At least someone thought this was a good plan,* Seb thought.

Sami and Seb packed up their fishing gear and left the camp. Rocky followed along behind, stopping to sniff at bushes or undergrowth. Every now and then, he'd catch sight of a squirrel and take off after it. Sami would call him back. Once she had to drag him away by his collar from a tree where he was sure he had a squirrel cornered.

"I'm not sure Rocky is going to be that helpful as our babysitter," Sami said.

"If you get mad at me for falling in the water, what are you going to do when Rocky jumps in?" Seb asked her.

"Hopefully we'll be able to get him to nap in the shade," Sami said. "Now where's this canyon you're talking about?"

They were walking along the edge of the river. It was thick with long green grass. Wildflowers—blue hare bells hanging in clusters, feathery purple asters, arnica like yellow stars—dotted the grasses.

BLUE HARE BELLS

PURPLE ASTERS

ARNICA

"Did you know having lots of wildflowers is a sign that there's been a lot of rain lately?" Seb said. "Wildflower seeds can just stay in the dirt for a long time until they feel like it's wet enough for them to grow."

"I've never seen so many in the mountains," Sami said. "We should pick some to make our dinner table look pretty."

"Dinner table?" Seb asked.

"Fine—dinner log," Sami said. "A dinner log full of freshly fried brook trout."

When they reached the canyon, its dirt and rock sides stretching steeply up from the water, Sami had to agree that it was a great fishing location.

"There's just enough room to cast along the bank," she said. "But the river is narrower so it makes it deeper. Fish like to hide in that deep water."

"I know," Seb said. "The current is slower in deep water so they don't have to swim as hard as where it's shallow. I read about it. Where are you going to fish? I don't think there's room for both of us to fish in the same spot."

Sami gave him a look that said she knew exactly what he was thinking.

"I'll go upstream," she said. "That way, if you fall in again, you won't ruin my fishing."

She stomped off up the bank. Rocky wandered along behind her. In a few minutes, they were both out of sight around a bend in the river.

Seb sat down on a rock and adjusted his glasses. This was what he had wanted—a chance to try fishing all on his own without anyone interfering.

It felt a little lonely, all the same, to have no one else in view. He reminded himself that Sami and Rocky were probably only around the bend. He could shout if he needed them.

He selected an elk hair caddis fly and attached it to his line. He'd read it was the best one for brook trout. It was supposed to rest on top of the water, not sink into it.

Like its name said, it was made of elk hair, a little tuft of grayish-brownish hair tied to a hook with coils of thread. Would it fool a brook trout into thinking it was a real caddis fly? Time to find out.

ELK HAIR CADDIS FLY

Seb stood on the edge of the bank. Looking upstream, he could see the pattern of the river. It leapt between rocks and then fell into pools. Fish might be in any of the places where the current slowed.

Seb scanned the river, following the flow down as it ducked beneath a steep bank, just above where he was standing. Here the water whirled into a small basin between some rocks. That's the spot, Seb thought. That's where he'd hide if he were a fish.

Seb held his rod out in front of him, pulling in any slack on the line. His thumb rested on top of the rod, where he could control the direction of a cast. He pulled his arm straight up, just behind his shoulder. The line zipped up and back. He flipped the rod forward to just a little in front of him and the line sailed past him.

He let more line out and then pulled his arm back up and then out again. Each time, he let out a little more line until it was swirling above him in a graceful arc. The trick was to keep it from going too far back, where the fly would catch in brush.

Now it was time. The next time his arm came forward, he brought it all the way forward and the line soared out over the water and dropped just below the pool under the bank. The lure rested on the water, floating slowly downstream.

Not far enough, Seb thought. He needed to get it into the pool.

He started carefully reeling his line in. It was important not to let his fly get too wet if he wanted to keep using it.

Time to cast again. He pulled the line taut again and then started to repeat the process of flinging it up in the air and out over the water.

The key thing was to stay calm. He realized he'd been holding his breath and let it out in a long sigh. Now he matched his breath to the motion of his cast. Up, breathe in. Forward, breathe out.

And then he cast. Again the line hung in the air for a moment and then the lure dropped into the water, into the pool.

Seb only had a moment to admire his cast before there was a ripple under the water and his fly was gone. Seb couldn't believe it. Had a fish just bitten his lure? He had to keep cool. Don't set the hook until the fish was heading back down into the water, he remembered from his book.

Well, it was heading down. He reeled in the line, just a little, until he could feel a tug. That was it, that was the fish, pulling on the hook. He reeled it tighter.

In a flash, the fish burst to the surface, trying to dash away from whatever was in its mouth. But it was too late. Seb reeled in quickly. The fish pulled desperately and Seb let the line play out some so he didn't accidentally tug the hook loose. But he was reeling in and slowly, he worked the line shorter and shorter.

He could see the fish now, darting in the shallows, thrashing with its tail as it tried to get free. Seb waded into the water and reeled in farther until the fish was right there at his feet. Seb bent down and put his hand around the slippery, wet fish.

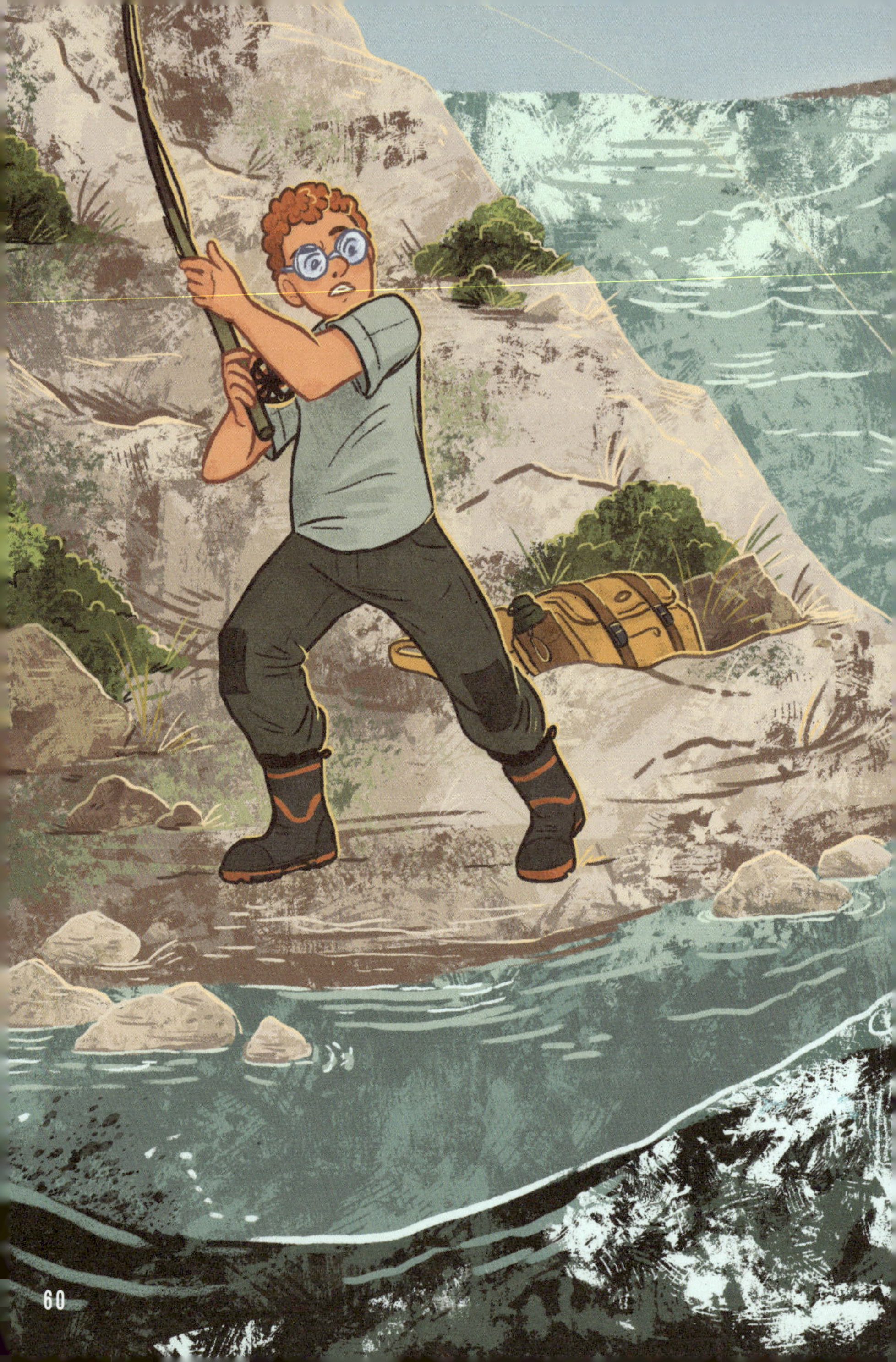

It was a brook trout, around ten inches long. It was speckled with yellow spots and pink spots encircled with blue. In Seb's hand, it thrashed, a hook lodged in the corner of its mouth.

"I caught a fish," Seb whispered to himself.

CHAPTER 6
CAUGHT!

The fish flapped its gills at him.

"I caught a fish!" This time Seb did not whisper.

He heard a rattle of stones behind him. Sami came running around the bend in the river, hopping from rock to rock in her hurry. She stopped short when she saw him standing in the river holding a fish. Rocky, running behind her, bumped his nose into her knee.

"No way!" Sami cried. "That's awesome, Seb!"

Rocky started bouncing through the water to get to Seb. Sami caught hold of his collar.

"You stay, Rock," she said. "This is not something you can help with. Go sit on the bank. Go! Sit!"

Sami gave the dog a gentle push to shore and then waded out into the water to Seb.

"What a gorgeous brookie, Seb," Sami said, touching its fins. "You did it! You're a real fisherman now."

Seb grinned. "Did you know I used an elk hair caddis fly like it said in my book?"

Sami laughed. "Good for your book. Now we should probably unhook this fish and get it back in the water before it suffocates in the air."

"But I don't want to release it," Seb protested. "I want to give it to my mom to make for dinner."

"I didn't mean release it. We'll string it and keep it alive in the water until it's time to clean it and eat it."

Sami pulled a fish stringer from her pocket. It was nothing more than a thin, strong nylon string with a metal section at one end, but it would keep the fish fresh in the water without letting it swim away.

Seb held the fish steady with one hand and with the other started to wiggle the hook out of its mouth. He nearly dropped it once, but had the hook free at last. He didn't like the feel of removing the hook, but this was part of fishing. He couldn't help but notice that his was the first fish on the stringer today; Sami hadn't caught one yet.

Sami slid the metal needle of the stringer through the fish's gills. "Now we'll tie this to a branch and keep it in the water while we keep fishing. Hopefully by the end of the day, we'll have a whole string full to take to Kathleen. "Because." She pretended to glare at Seb. "Don't think you'll be the only one catching fish today."

They tied the stringer to a tree branch that overhung the bank, so that the fish stayed in the water. Rocky had tried to help again with securing the stringer, but Sami sternly ordered him back to the riverbank. He lay there now with his nose pillowed on his paws and his red floppy ears falling beside it. He looked very sad.

"No matter how sad you look, you still can't fish, Rocky," Sami said. She waved goodbye to Seb and headed back up the canyon, clearly determined to catch her own fish right away.

Seb stopped to rub Rocky's ears. "Not much fun for you, is it Rocky?" he said. The dog leaned into him and Seb took a minute to sit on the riverbank. His feet still needed to warm up from standing in the cold river. It was nice to rest in the sun and let his mind run over all the moments of successfully catching his first fish.

But he didn't rest long. He knew it would not be long before Sami caught one, too. He wanted to take a bunch of fish home at the end of the day, not just one. He made sure his fly was still firmly attached to the fishing line and headed back out to the water.

Now he felt like he had the motion down. Arm up, arm forward, up and forward, get the line swirling over his head. And cast, shooting the line out over the water.

He did not get any interest from the fish in the same hole the first few times he cast into it. He wandered a little farther upstream. Rocky lifted his head to watch Seb walk along, but he didn't follow.

Seb watched the sun glint off the river. It was hard to tell with all the light on the water where there were deeper holes that fish might be hiding in. He picked a spot where the current looked calmer just below a big rock. He could see dirty foam floating in an eddy where the water ran into the pool.

Just the place for flies to wash downstream, he thought.

Seb started casting again. He didn't get the fly close to the pool. It landed in shallower water. He reeled it back in and was just about to start casting again when he looked up to see Sami watching him. She held up her own pole with a fish on the line.

"We're even!" she called. She headed downstream to where they'd tied the stringer.

Sami caught two more that morning. Seb caught one more, though it wasn't as big as the first one. After a while, they stopped to snack on granola bars and drink bottled water.

While they rested, they let Rocky go run around and play in the river since he'd been so good waiting on the shore all morning. Rocky's idea of fishing was to jump into the river and bite the water ferociously. He shook his coat and water splashed all over them.

"Rocky!" they both yelled.

"Although, it is a hot day, isn't it? I don't mind getting a little wet." Sami added.

"It looks like clouds are coming, though," said Seb. He pointed up over the ridge to the mountains. The sky was darker there and gray clouds were starting to form.

"Hmm," Sami said. "Well I guess it will be cooler without the sun. We should keep an eye on it though."

It was not just cooler without the sun, but also easier to see into the water without sun reflecting off of it. As the cloud cover increased, Seb could see fish lurking in the shadowy water. He caught another one and then joined Sami walking farther into the canyon to find more good fishing holes.

Sami paused by the river to look up at the clouds over the mountains.

"I'm not sure about those clouds, Seb," she said. "They look pretty dark. It may mean rain."

"Will rain make it so we can't fish?" Seb asked. "Does it scare the fish away?"

"Oh you can fish in the rain," Sami said. "I mean, fish don't mind getting wet."

Seb laughed.

"I was just thinking about what that ranger said. About flash flooding," Sami said.

Seb looked up at the darkened sky. They were too tucked into the canyon to get a good view of any coming weather changes. All they could see were the clouds themselves.

"It's a long way from here," Seb said. "Wouldn't Carlos come get us if it looked like bad weather?"

"Maybe he can't see it from where they are at the lake," Sami said.

"Well anyway," Seb said. "I want to catch more fish! Then we can go back."

He stepped out into the river and pulled up his rod, ready to start casting. Sami stood looking at the clouds a moment longer, then shrugged and followed Seb's example.

They didn't notice Rocky start to sniff at the ground, his ears perked up at attention.

Seb cast his line out over the water. He saw the fly float on the water for a moment and then bob as something disturbed it from below. He waited, holding his breath, hoping the fish would take another bite and be hooked.

And then Rocky started barking, loud and sharp, right behind him.

CHAPTER 7
IN A FLASH

Seb jumped at the sound and jerked his rod up. The fly flipped into the air. There was a whirl in the water and the fish was gone.

"Rocky!" Seb yelled. "What are you doing?"

Rocky continued to bark. He pawed at the ground and gave a little whine.

Sami came over to where Seb and Rocky stood. "What's wrong, Rocky?" she said.

"What's wrong is he messed up my fishing," Seb said. "I almost had one and he started barking and now it's gone. Silly dog. We should have left you at camp."

Rocky shoved his head at Sami's legs and whined again.

"No," Sami said. "Something's wrong. Is it an animal, Rocky?"

Seb remembered mountain wildcats and bears and looked fearfully up the canyon walls to the pine trees. As he looked up, he saw that the clouds that had rolled in looked gloomy and heavy with rain.

"Sami," he said. "I think it might be raining over the mountains."

Sami looked up quickly. Wind rushed through the trees high above them, fast and wild. The tall pine trees creaked and swayed in the sudden gust.

"I think you're right," she said, frowning. "I don't like this, Seb, and I don't think Rocky does either. If it rains upstream, this river could flood, really quickly."

"A flash flood?" Seb remembered that he had never asked Carlos what they should do if the river flooded.

Sami nodded. "The ranger said the ground was already wet from lots of rain, remember? And this area is really rocky so it's not like it can absorb a lot of rain. If there's a bunch of rain in the mountains and it all washes down in this river . . ."

Rocky barked again.

"OK," Sami said. "Rocky is right. There is something wrong and we need to get out of here. The water will rise in this canyon faster than anywhere."

"Should we go back downstream?" Seb asked. He suddenly wished he knew more about fishing in Wyoming than he'd read in his book. Nothing in his book had mentioned what to do in this situation.

Sami wasn't listening to him. She was looking upstream and listening, her head tilted on one side. Rocky was doing the same thing. If Seb hadn't been scared, it would have been funny to see them in the same position.

Then he heard what Sami had already identified. A rumbling sound.

"We have to go," Sami said. "Come on."

"Back to camp?" Seb asked.

"No time. We have to get out of this canyon. We have to go up."

They were standing on the rocky edge of the riverbank. Behind them, the canyon wall rose abruptly. But across the river, the slope was less steep, with bushes and grass growing in clumps between large boulders. Sami grabbed Seb's arm and pulled him into the river, running for the opposite shore.

"Climb," she shouted. "Up the slope now!"

"We can't climb that!" Seb said. "It's basically a cliff."

"We can climb from rock to rock. And we have to. By the time we got down this canyon, it might be too late. Those rocks are steep, but if we can get up them, we'll be safe on the ridge," Sami said.

Rocky followed Sami without being asked. The dog jumped up one rock and then scrambled onto the next, his nails scraping a little against the hard surface as he went. Sami started climbing as soon as she reached the other bank.

Seb ran to catch up, splashing through the water. Sami was already shouting at him from on top of a boulder, so he couldn't stop to think about it.

Reaching the canyon's edge, he easily climbed the first few loose boulders. Looking up, though, he could see they got steeper and more scattered. How could he make it up that whole slope?

"Come on, Seb!" Sami yelled.

The rushing, rumbling sound was getting louder. Sami was right. There was no alternative but to get out of the canyon in the most direct way.

Seb jumped onto the next big rock and then quickly hopped to another. His foot landed on the side of it and he bobbled, struggling to keep his balance. He reached out and grabbed at the rock with one hand. He still held his fishing rod in the other hand. Should he just drop it? He didn't want to lose his brand-new fishing rod that he'd only just learned to use.

He jumped again, this time more carefully, to land on the next boulder. Looking over at Sami, he could see she was holding her fishing rod still, too. He paused, breathing hard, and looked back at the river. Was the level higher? He couldn't tell.

"Keep going, Seb," Sami said. Her voice was calm but serious. "It's just rock hopping. Just like we did when we forded the river when we hiked in. Just jump from one rock to the next."

She had moved closer to him, waiting to make sure he was coming. Seb found a foothold on a smaller rock to help him jump up to the next one. He was nervous, but if Sami was going to wait for him, he had to hustle so she wouldn't be in danger either.

The river would churn fast through a canyon because there was nowhere else for the water to go. No plants or dirt to slow it down and absorb it. Nothing but more rock to bounce off.

Rain started to fall. Just a few drops at first, landing lightly on Seb's back and neck. Then they were blowing into his face and spotting his glasses. Rocky barked and growled.

"It's going to get slippery," Seb shouted.

"Then we have to just go faster," she yelled. "Let's tie our fishing rods to our packs. Then we can move more quickly."

They were getting higher up the riverbank. Rocky was ahead of them, but he kept coming back to bark at them. He nudged his nose behind Seb's legs like he was pushing him to go faster.

At last they came to the edge of the boulder field. Seb used a few clumps of grass and some scraggly bushes to pull himself along. He even found a small pine tree and used that like a pole to push himself upward.

Sami reached the edge of the ridge first and pulled herself over the top under the pine trees. She grabbed hold of Seb's shirt and helped him scramble up beside her.

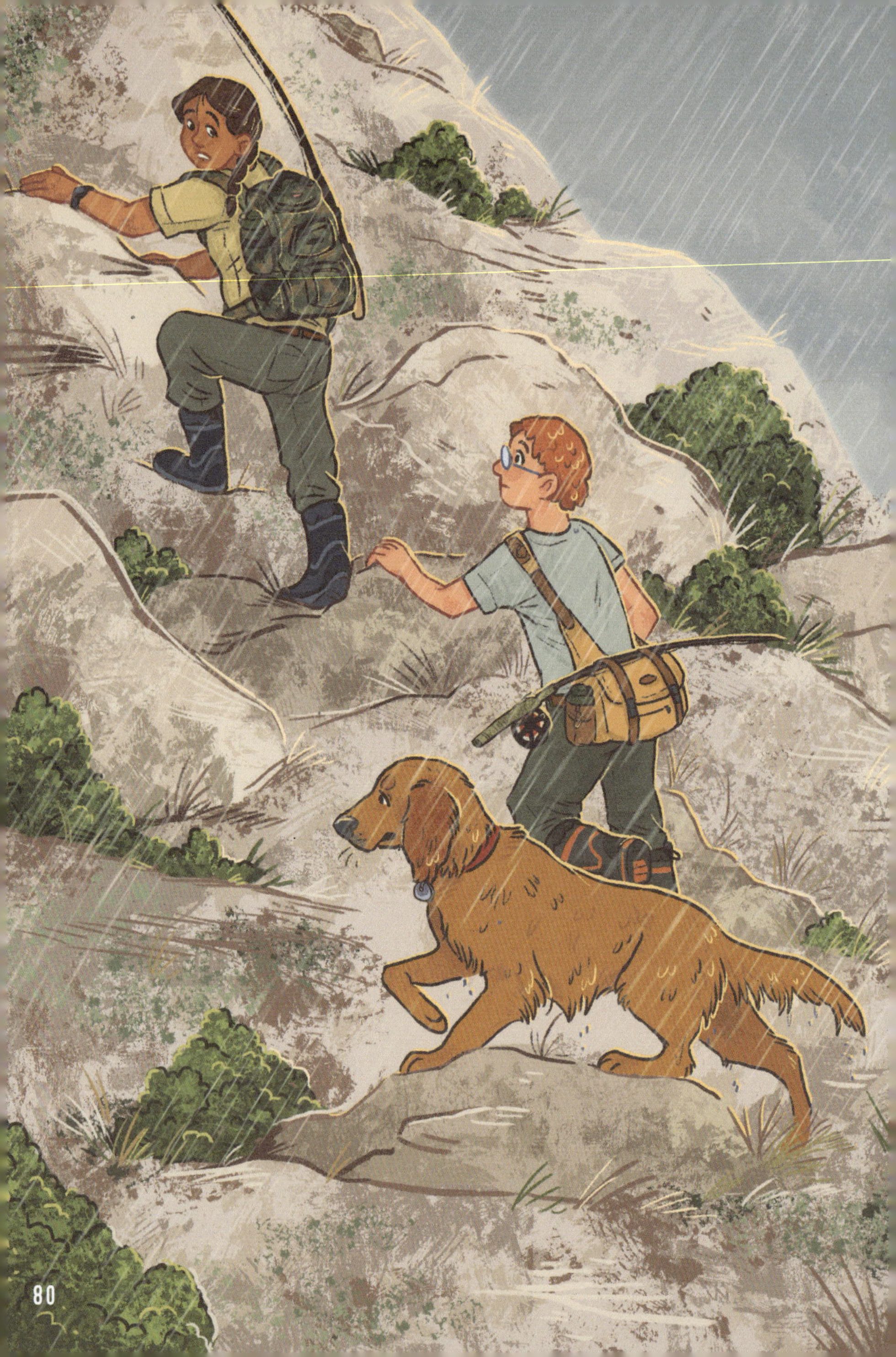

Rocky had beaten them to the top and came running to meet them.

"Good job, Rocky," Sami said. "You made it and we're all here now."

Rocky panted and licked her hands. Seb reached over and patted him on the head. Then Seb sat down under the trees and looked back down at the river they had fled.

The water level was already higher. He could tell that easily by seeing where he had been standing on the opposite bank below. Those rocks were covered, but not by much. Sami sat down beside him.

"It doesn't look too bad," Seb said. He took his glasses off and wiped them clean on his damp shirt.

Then, as they watched, the river changed. The gentle burble of flowing water turned into a roar. The river level rose abruptly, tumbling and thrashing through the canyon.

The river pounded off the rocks and sprayed into the air. The still pools where they had caught trout were covered in wild rapids. In minutes, the canyon floor was completely underwater.

CHAPTER 8
SMELLS LIKE WET DOG

"Wow," Sami whispered.

They stared down at the flooded river where they had been fishing only a few moments before.

"I didn't really think it could happen that fast," Seb said. "I mean, it wasn't even raining here until a few minutes ago."

"It's the rain upstream that matters for a flash flood," Sami said. "When it pours up high, it comes down in a rush. This canyon

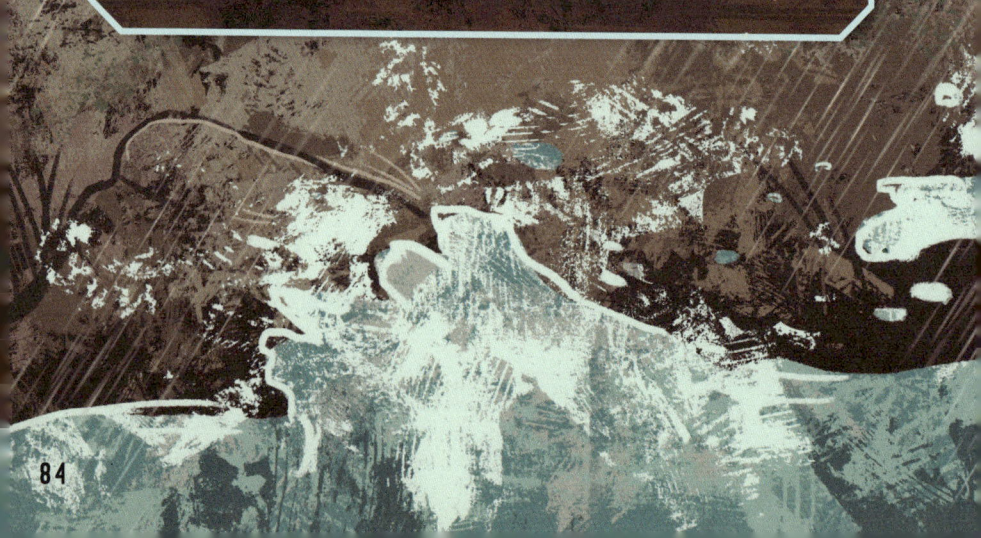

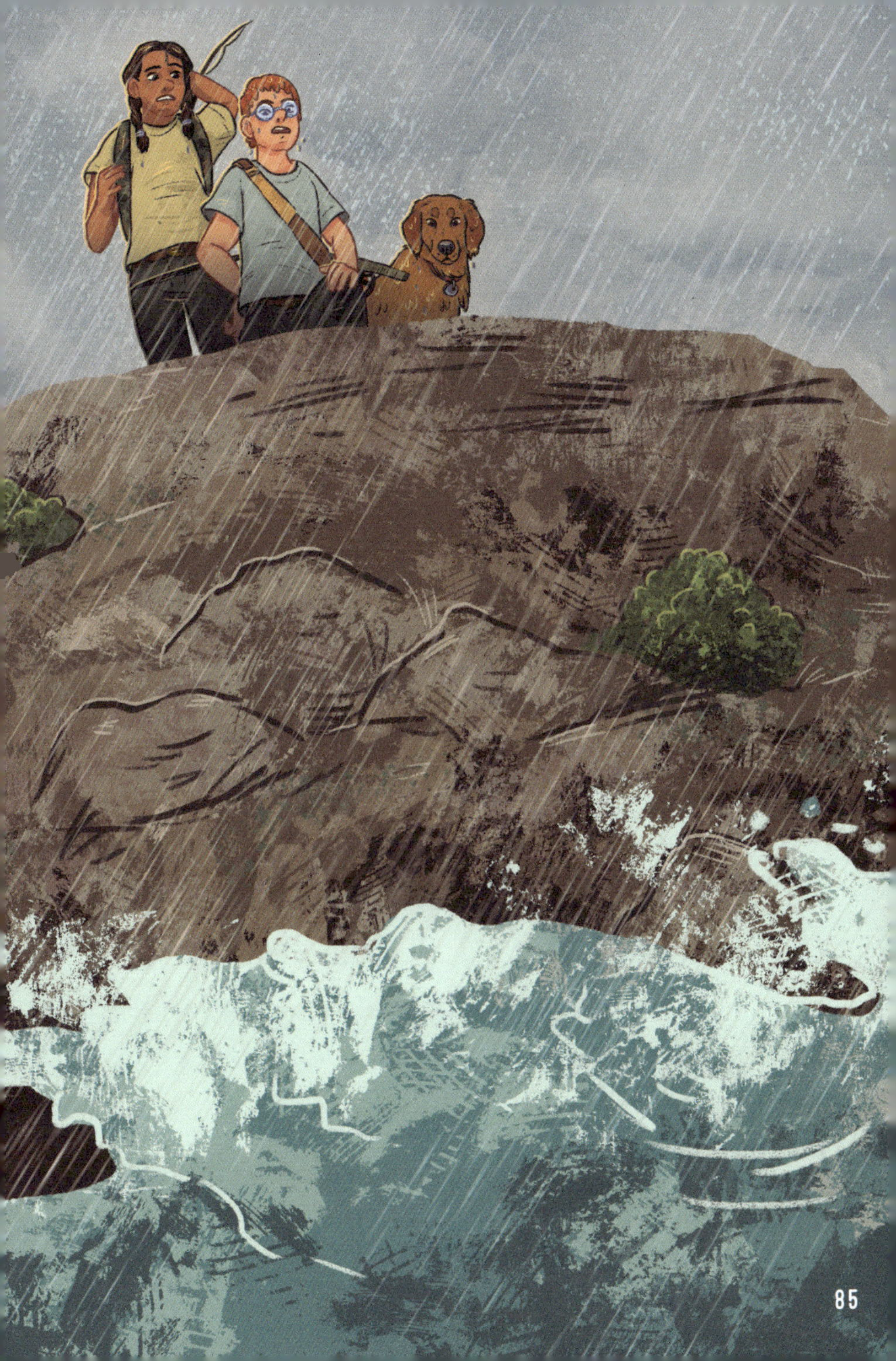

is so narrow and rocky that it forces all the water together. Farther down, like by the meadow, it might not even flood too badly, just get higher on the banks and maybe wash over a few little islands in the river."

The noise the river was making was tremendous. They had to sit close together to hear each other speak. Seb was kind of glad Sami was close, though he wouldn't tell her that.

"How did you know it was going to flood?" Seb asked.

"Well, I didn't really know for sure. But I saw something like this once when I was camping in Colorado with my dad a few years ago. One minute it was a nice day and then the next minute the river was a mess," she said.

"It was a good thing you were here," Seb

muttered. "I mean, I guess I've read about flash floods, but I didn't know how to tell."

Sami smiled at him. "Rocky helped," she said. "I might not have made us go so quickly if he hadn't been upset. I guess he could hear it coming before we could."

Rocky, hearing his name, sat down behind them so he could squeeze his head in between them and rest it on both their knees. His tail thumped the dirt behind him.

"Good job, Rock," Seb said, and rubbed his ears.

The rain was coming down harder now. Seb's shirt was soaked. Pine trees didn't offer much rain protection.

"Do you think we'll be OK up here?" Seb asked.

"We're pretty high up," Sami noted. "And the river would have to wash away all those huge boulders before it got to us."

"How long will we be stuck here?" Seb asked.

Suddenly he realized that *stuck* was the right word. They were on the opposite side of the river from their camp and from Carlos and Kathleen. There was no way for them to cross a river this high.

"I'm not sure," Sami said. "The flood won't last forever though, Seb. I mean, the rain will stop and then the water will go down. Maybe not immediately, but it'll happen. Then we can worry about finding our way back to camp."

She nudged him with her shoulder. "Anyway, we're together and now we can talk about which of us is the better fisherman."

Seb grinned. "That'll be a short conversation, because it's me. Mainly I'm worried because this spot is starting to smell like wet dog."

Sami laughed. "Good point. Let's go explore instead. Maybe we'll find a better place to cross the river when the water starts to go down."

They both scrambled to their feet, being careful to stay back from the edge of the ridge. Staying among the pines so they were well above the canyon, Sami took the lead in their exploring. Seb didn't argue with her about it. It was nice to have someone there who seemed to know what to do.

The ridge climbed to the top of a little hill and then started to drop closer to the river bank below them. Seb looked down at the river, the water was still high and rushing.

"Look!" Sami said.

While Seb had been looking down, she had been looking up. Seb followed her pointing finger and found what she'd seen. Over the mountains, the sky was clearing.

They could see blue through the clouds and even a touch of sunshine.

"If this rainstorm just keeps rolling on through, the rain will let up and the flood will go down," Sami said.

"Hey Sami, what happens to the fish when it floods? I didn't see anything about that in my book," he said.

"Huh. Actually I have no idea," she said. "Let's ask my dad."

He didn't like to say so, but Seb was pretty anxious to see his mom and Carlos, and not just to ask them questions about fish. He knew they hadn't been near the river today, but he still wanted to make sure they were okay.

Sami and Seb followed the sloping ridge away from their fishing canyon until they reached a spot Seb recognized—this was where he had stomped off to when he got mad at Sami on their first day of fishing.

"If we go down here, this is right across the river from the camp," he said.

"Let's go carefully. If the flood washed over the bank here, it could have knocked over trees or even changed the riverbed," Sami said.

The ridge was lower than the canyon and they were already closer to the water. What had yesterday been a big ell bend in the river, though, was now running with extra water.

Rain splashed down on its surface. Seb and Sami came as close as they could to the new bank of the river and looked across to where they could just see part of their tent through the trees on the opposite side. The river between them and the camp was flooded, deep and fast moving.

There was no way for them to get across.

CHAPTER 9
IT'S GEOLOGY

"Samantha! Sebastian!"

The shout came from across the river and they looked up to see Carlos and Kathleen running from the camp to the river. Carlos kept yelling their names and Kathleen looked like she was crying.

"Hi Dad! Hi Kathleen!" Sami shouted.

"We're over here!" Seb yelled.

Carlos and Kathleen stopped running and started waving at them. Kathleen was definitely crying, but she was also smiling.

"We're all right, Kathleen," Sami shouted. Rocky barked. "Rocky's all right, too."

Carlos wiped rain off his face. He looked tired and Seb wondered if they had run all the way from the lake.

"We didn't see the rain coming from where we were at the lake," Carlos said. He had to yell to be heard across the river. "We didn't know until the clouds came in over us and it started raining. Then we ran up to the canyon to try to get you. And we didn't see you . . . and the canyon is badly flooded."

Kathleen gave a little sob. "Are you sure you're OK?" she said.

"Well I'm fine and so are Sami and Rocky," Seb said. "Don't worry, Mom. But Carlos, what happens to all the fish when the river floods? Do they get washed downstream?"

Carlos had been close to crying himself, but now he almost laughed. "You know, Seb, I think we might discuss that another time. Right now I'm more anxious to find out what happens to kids when the river floods. Sami, you can't cross right now."

Sami and Seb looked at each other and rolled their eyes. Parents. Did they think their teenagers were five years old?

"I know, Dad," Sami said. "We have to wait until the rain stops and river level goes down and then see if it's safe to cross. We know that."

It was hard to see for sure across the flood river, but Seb thought Kathleen and Carlos looked at each other and rolled their eyes, too.

"OK, Sami," Carlos said. "But you two stay where we can see you."

Kathleen sat down on a fallen log near the riverbank and stared over at them like she was never going to take her eyes off them again.

Sami sighed. "I guess we'd better make ourselves comfortable, Seb," she said. "And I'm pretty sure we'll not get to go fishing by ourselves again for a while."

Sami, Seb, and Rocky found a cluster of pine trees a few feet back from the river and sat down to wait out the flood.

"How long will we have to sit here?" Seb asked Sami.

Sami shrugged. "It could take a while, Seb. Like, hours even. I don't know how much rain came down over the mountains and it's still raining here."

As she spoke, however, a little ray of sunlight suddenly broke through the dark clouds. The rain was slowing. Like many afternoon mountain thunderstorms, this one had moved in fast and out fast, though the mess left behind would last longer.

Seb's wet shirt felt glued to his skin. He tried to dry his glasses on it, but they just smudged with more water.

"Did you know high water levels can change the course of a river?" he said to Sami.

"Did you read that in your book about Wyoming?" she said.

"No, I learned that in school. It's geology."

Sami laughed. "I don't know whether a flash flood like this will have changed the river bed that much, but it definitely knocked over some smaller trees and bushes and stuff in its path. We'll probably have to find some new place to cross it because the old fords might be moved around."

They both looked down at the river in front of them, the stretch they had fished their first afternoon camping. Seb wondered if the fly he lost that day, tangled in a piece of driftwood, had drifted on downstream when the flooding started.

Then the water had been crystal clear

and he could see every rock in its path. Now it was muddy with churned up dirt and he couldn't even see the bottom. They couldn't wade through it today.

"Hello there!" Sami and Seb jumped at the shout from behind them. Rocky leaped to his feet and started barking.

Standing on the top of the ridge above them was the ranger they had met on their hike out. He was standing next to his horse and waving down at them.

"Did you get stuck on the wrong side of the river when the flooding started, too?" Seb called. He and Sami stood up and started climbing up to meet him.

"It came up quickly, didn't it?" the ranger said. "I was up higher today looking over the trail farther into the mountains. I thought I'd check on you folks on my way back, though it took me a while to find you."

"We were fishing in that canyon upstream when the flash flood started," Seb said. "We had to climb up a bunch of boulders to get away in time and now we can't get back across the river to the camp."

Seb pointed across the river to where Carlos and Kathleen were now standing and waving to the ranger.

"You were smart to get out of the canyon," said the ranger, waving back at their parents.

"Sami made us move fast," Seb said.

"I had seen a flash flood before," Sami said.

"So you knew what to do," the ranger smiled at her. "But now you're stuck over here away from your parents. Well, I may have a solution for you. Want to come check out what I found a little farther downstream?"

The ranger waved his arms at Carlos and Kathleen and pointed downstream.

Then he started down the ridge toward the meadow. As they came down off the ridge to the meadow they found that the flood had knocked loose an old dead tree so that it now lay across the river, a natural bridge.

"Can we walk across it?" Sami asked eagerly.

"Carefully," the ranger nodded. "I'm going to tie a rope around each of you while you take turns walking across. Let's get you back to your parents."

"And our food," said Seb. "All I've had since breakfast is a granola bar."

Rocky barked in agreement. Across the river, Carlos and Kathleen had come around from the other side and were waiting by the log.

The ranger tied a loop of rope around Sami's waist. "If you fall, I'll still have ahold of you."

"I won't fall," Sami said confidently. She climbed up on the log. It was big and wide. A few broken branches stood up along its length, so she could hold onto them as she crossed, but she didn't need to. She held her fishing pole in one hand and easily hopped off the trunk on the other bank.

Carlos was waiting with a huge hug. Then he untied the rope from her waist and the ranger pulled it back across the river.

"Your turn now," he said to Seb. "You ready?"

Seb looked down at the muddy water and then across the river at Sami.

"How long do you think it will take for the flood to go down?" he asked.

"Oh that can be hours," the ranger said. "It'll probably be back to normal by the morning and then the fish will be out and biting again."

That reminded Seb of the really important question. "What happens to fish when it floods? Do they get washed away? Will we even be able to find any here tomorrow?"

"The fish will still be here," said the ranger. "They'll find a spot out of the strong current, like a little side channel or a deep section or in back of a rock."

Finally, the answer to his question! And he was pleased to hear that there would still be fish around in the morning. He used a branch to pull himself onto the log and stepped out over the river. Rocky hopped onto the log behind him.

Going slowly, grabbing at the branches along the length of the log, he inched his way across the river. Below him, the water was starting to look a little less wild. He was definitely glad he wasn't a fish trying to find a safe spot in this water though.

When Seb reached the other side, Kathleen grabbed ahold of him and Carlos untied the rope from his waist.

"Thank you!" they all yelled at the ranger. He waved back and, gathering up the rope, started leading his horse back to the trail.

"I hope he can get back OK," Seb said. "Hey Mom, guess what—I caught three fish this morning."

Kathleen was still hugging him and Sami together. "Well that's nice, but it's nicer to have you both back safe," she said. Rocky nudged up against them, trying to get inside the hug, too.

Then Seb realized. "Sami! What happened to our fish we caught?"

CHAPTER 10
HUGS AND FISHES

"Oh no, I totally forgot about them!" Sami cried. "Dad, we've got to find our fish! We left them on a stringer in the river."

Carlos laughed. "I think the kids are okay if they've still got fish on their minds, Kath," he said. "But no, Sami, we are not going to go hunt for your fish in a flooded river today, no matter how amazing they were. We'll go after them tomorrow."

Seb groaned. "I was looking forward to fish for dinner," he said. "I'm starving."

"Well I've got you covered there, as long as you don't mind cutthroats instead of brookies," Carlos said.

"Dad, you caught some in the lake?" Sami said. "Can we see them?"

Kathleen sighed. "You all are fish crazy. Yes, let's go back to camp. I am ready to get into some dry clothes and I'll bet the rest of you are, too."

"The rain is letting up," Carlos said. "I'll be able to get a fire going and we can all dry out."

They walked back to the camp together. Seb and Sami told their parents about how they'd seen the storm clouds over the mountain and about Rocky barking. Seb gave Sami full credit for knowing that they had to act fast getting out of the canyon to higher ground. She gave him a little sideways smile. Seb grinned back.

Carlos and Kathleen said they had been busy fishing at the lake when the rain started. They were surrounded by trees that blocked their view of the horizon so they hadn't seen the clouds rolling in until the sun was hidden and the rain had started. Then they, like Sami, had remembered what the ranger had said about flash flooding.

They thought of Sami and Seb and Rocky, fishing in a canyon where the water would rise fastest. They had run up to the ridge above the canyon and seen the flood filling the canyon floor.

"We couldn't see you," said Kathleen, her voice a little quavery. "I guess you were just across the river, exploring the ridge, but we couldn't see you at all."

Seb patted her back. "It's OK, Mom. We're all fine now except maybe our fish."

Carlos's fish were waiting for them back at the camp: four big cutthroat trout. Seb admired their speckled backs and the red patch just below their gills that gave them their nickname.

"The fish Seb and I caught were much

bigger, but these will work," Sami teased Carlos. "Let's clean them and we can eat!"

Seb hadn't cleaned fish before and wasn't sure he wanted to learn. But Carlos said that knowing how to treat the fish you were going to eat was part of the responsibility of a fisherman.

"Usually I'd clean these in the river, but we're going to keep away from that wild water for now. We have a jug full of water here in the camp and we will use that for washing our hands," Carlos said.

Carlos showed Seb how to slit the fish's belly open with a knife, starting from where the tail began up to just below its jaw bone. Carlos was able to pull the fish guts out from the cut with one quick motion. It took Seb a few tries to pull it all clear and it was definitely messy. Sami had done a neater job with the trout she was cleaning.

"It just takes practice," she said to Seb. He rolled his eyes. There were so many things to practice around Sami!

Cleaning their hands without the benefit of the river to quickly rinse everything away was challenging, but when they felt relatively free of fish, Sami and Seb took turns changing in the tent. Kathleen had gotten dry clothes for herself already. Now she had the camp stove open and was warming a bit of butter in the pan.

Carlos dried off, too, and then got to work starting a fire. With the ground so wet, it was harder to start than usual, but he had saved some firewood under a tarp beside the tent just in case.

Carlos split a few of the larger logs into kindling and then stacked them in the fire ring with the big logs on top. In a few minutes, smoke was pouring out of the middle of the stack and then flames started to lick up the sides of the big logs.

Seb sniffed the air. There was a nice wet smell of damp pine trees and grass and now the smell of the fire with it. This was one of his favorite things about camping—the way his hair and clothes would smell like campfire for the whole trip.

Now the camp started to smell like fish. Kathleen had slid two of the big cutthroat trout into the pan and was rolling them around in butter as they browned.

"I know it's not dinnertime and I haven't made anything to go with the fish yet, but we all missed a real lunch and these will be at their best if we eat them at their freshest!" she said.

"And to think I teased you about carrying butter in your pack," Carlos said. He put his arm around her and leaned in to kiss her.

"Gross!" Sami and Seb shouted together.

Kathleen laughed and served a fish each for Sami and Seb before sitting down with her hot tea. Carlos cooked the second two fish.

Seb ate his with his fingers, pulling chunks of fish from the bones and dropping them straight into his mouth. Rocky had been lying by the fire, warming his fur. At the smell of food, he got up and came to stand by Sami, hoping she might drop something.

"These are really good," Seb said to Sami. "But I'll bet mine would have tasted better."

"You know the flood probably washed away the whole stringer, right?" Sami said.

"I know those are probably gone, but did you know I asked the ranger and he said the fish in the river probably hid from the flood so they'll still be there tomorrow?" Seb said.

"I'm ready for them," said Sami, with determination.

Sami took another bite of fish and then dropped a small piece into Rocky's mouth. Rocky wagged his tail enthusiastically. Seb was licking butter off his fingers. Carlos was just finishing up his and Kathleen's early fish dinner.

The wood crackled and snapped in the fire ring. Above them, the sky was now clear and blue, just beginning to darken for the evening. In the distance, Seb could hear the river. It sounded louder than usual, but he was sure the water was going down now. The fish would be swimming out of hiding, looking for their own evening meal.

Tomorrow, Seb would be ready for them, too.

112